# Disney's Princess Collection

*Love & Friendship Stories*

SCHOLASTIC INC.

New York  Toronto  London  Auckland  Sydney
Mexico City  New Delhi  Hong Kong

# TABLE OF CONTENTS

# TABLE OF CONTENTS

Written by Sarah E. Heller
Designed by Todd Taliaferro

This edition containing the full text of *Bambi, A Life in the Woods* by Felix Salten
is published by Simon & Schuster.
Tarzan® owned by Edgar Rice Burroughs, Inc. and Used by Permission.
© Edgar Rice Burroughs, Inc. and Disney Enterprises, Inc.

ISBN 0-439-22154-4

 Published by Scholastic Inc., 555 Broadway, New York, NY 10012,
 by arrangement with Disney Press, an imprint of Buena Vista Books, Inc.
SCHOLASTIC and associated logos are trademarks and/or
registered trademarks of Scholastic Inc.

12  11  10  9  8  7  6                    3  4  5/0

Printed in the U.S.A.                     24

First Scholastic printing, September 2000

This book is set in 20-point Cochin.

# Walt Disney's

# Cinderella

## The Mice Save the Day

Cinderella imagined herself dancing at the royal ball as she held her mother's old dress against her. It needed a few alterations, but they wouldn't be difficult, if only she could find the time to do them.

"Cinderellllaa!" yelled her stepmother and stepsisters again. They were getting ready for the ball and they wouldn't give Cinderella a moment's peace.

"I guess my dress will just have to wait," the poor girl sighed.

As she left the room, Jaq, one of Cinderella's favorite mouse friends, said, "Know what? Cinderelly not go to the ball." The other mice looked at him, startled.

"Work, work, work!" he explained with disgust. "She never get dress done."

Cinderella's animal friends decided to surprise her by fixing the dress. After all, she had been caring for them for years. Just that day she had rescued poor Gus from a mousetrap. Then she had dressed him, fed him, and protected him from her stepmother's mean cat. So, together with the birds, her attic family lifted ribbons and scissors and sewing needles to help make

Cinderella's dream come true.

"Oh, thank you so much!" the beautiful girl exclaimed

when she saw what her friends had done for her. The

birds and mice were overjoyed to see Cinderelly so happy.
She deserved to have a special evening. Never
complaining for all she had to endure from her stepsisters
and stepmother, Cinderella still hoped that one day she

would find true happiness.

However, it was not long before her stepmother and

stepsisters took hope

away from her, too.

Tearing her beautiful

dress to shreds, they

left her alone,

sobbing in the

garden.

"There, there,"

soothed a new voice.

Cinderella's fairy

godmother magically appeared. "Dry your tears," she said. "You can't go to the ball looking like that."

Cinderella started to explain that she wasn't going to the ball, but her fairy godmother wouldn't hear of it.

Waving her magic wand, she turned a pumpkin into a

magnificent coach.

Cinderella and her animal friends stared at the magic

in amazement. "Bibbidi Bobbidi Boo!" sang the fairy

godmother. Soon, four of the mice, including Gus and Jaq, were turned into proud horses.

As for Cinderella, her new gown shimmered like

diamonds. She stood staring at her image in the fountain with disbelief.

"It's more than I ever hoped for!" she declared, her eyes sparkling.

When she arrived at the palace, Cinderella was swept into a dream world.

As she and the Prince swirled around the dance floor, everybody turned to stare at the beautiful girl who had caught the Prince's eye.

"Who is she?" they asked. "She must be a princess."

None could have imagined that earlier that day she had

been dressed in rags.

Never had Cinderella known such happiness! As the handsome young prince bowed before her, she felt her heart pounding. They danced together in the castle garden, swept up in the splendor of the evening.

Gazing into her eyes, the Prince leaned to kiss her just as the clock struck twelve. When she heard the bell toll, Cinderella remembered

her fairy godmother's warning that the spell would be broken at midnight. She raced down the grand staircase, leaving behind one of her dainty glass slippers.

The next day, doing her chores again, the young girl hummed dreamily. Realizing that Cinderella was the Prince's mysterious love, her stepmother mercilessly locked her in

her attic room.

"No! Please let me out," cried Cinderella. She knew that the Grand Duke was trying the glass slipper on every maiden in the kingdom. He would be here soon.

"We've just got to get that key," Jaq told Gus. Despite the danger, they pulled the key out of the stepmother's pocket, then pushed and pulled it up the long staircase. With a last

burst of energy, Cinderella's exhausted little friends were

finally able to slip the key under her locked door.

"Oh, thank you!" she cried.

Hurrying down the steps, Cinderella heard a crash. The

slipper she had left
behind was broken!
Pulling the other
slipper out of her
pocket, she called to the
Grand Duke, "May I
try this one on?"

The perfect fit proved that Cinderella was indeed the young woman who had won the Prince's heart.

Jaq and Gus cheered happily for their beautiful friend Cinderelly as they watched her dreams come true.

# Walt Disney's Sleeping Beauty

## THE FRIENDSHIP OF FAIRIES

In a magical kingdom there lived three kind and gentle fairies: Flora, Fauna, and Merryweather. Together, they worked to bring forth beauty, happiness, and love. Only by the power of their friendship could they defeat

the evil power of their rival, Maleficent.

One day after Maleficent cursed the infant Princess Aurora with a powerful spell, the

three good fairies secretly conspired to protect the innocent baby. "Maleficent doesn't know anything about love or kindness or the joy of helping others," Fauna reminded her friends.

This thought gave Flora an idea. Maleficent would never expect them to live like peasants and raise the child

themselves. Fauna was overjoyed with the proposal, but Merryweather, being the practical one, was reluctant to give up her wand.

"We've never done anything without magic before," she complained. But Flora insisted that they could do it if they worked together.

With love, they cared for the beautiful princess as if she were their own daughter. For fifteen years they kept her hidden in a cottage in the woods. Then, on the afternoon before her sixteenth birthday, the good fairies sent Briar Rose, as they had named her, to pick berries so that they could

plan a special surprise for her. Although they were sad about returning her to the King and Queen at sunset, they were content thinking about her future happiness.

Aurora sang as she gathered berries. She had the voice

of an angel, and the squirrels and birds and other woodland animals came to listen. She told them her dream of meeting a handsome stranger and falling in love.

Nearby, Prince Phillip was riding his horse, Samson. Hearing Aurora's beautiful singing, he asked, "What do you think it is? A wood sprite, maybe?" He was so

entranced by her song that he promised Samson a carrot

if he would follow the music. Excited, the horse galloped

too fast, knocking his friend off into a stream.

"No carrots for you!" said the Prince.

Seeing the wet clothes, some rabbits and an owl decided to play a game with Briar Rose. Laughing, she danced with her make-believe stranger until she realized

that a real man
had taken the
place of her
woodland
friends. As she
backed away,
Prince Phillip
called after her,

"But I'm not a stranger. We've met before."

He reminded her of the song she had been singing:
"You said so yourself . . . 'once upon a dream.'"

Looking at him closely, Aurora felt that she really did

know him. His smile made her trust him, and she held his hand as they danced and walked through the magnificent forest. With a gentle touch and a tender look, they knew in a moment that this was a love as strong and true as one could ever be.

"This is the happiest day of my life," Briar Rose

proclaimed when she returned to the cottage. However,

Flora, Fauna, and Merryweather were not pleased to

hear about her handsome stranger. As they explained that

she was a princess, Aurora fell into despair.  She thought

that she would never see her love again.

Sadly, the fairies led the Princess to her castle home, but they didn't realize that Maleficent had discovered them and was waiting to carry out her curse. As Aurora pricked her finger on the spindle of the spinning wheel and the whole castle fell into a deep sleep,

the good fairies realized that only the kiss of true love

would awaken the sleeping beauty.

Upon discovering that Prince Phillip was the stranger that

Aurora had met in the woods, they raced to Maleficent's castle and rescued him from her dungeon. The three fairies combined their powers of goodness in a fatal blow to the evil Maleficent. "Sword of truth, fly swift and sure, that evil die

and good endure." Their spell, combined with Prince Phillip's strength of heart, put an end to the ferocious dragon that Maleficent had become.

Awakened by a tender kiss, Princess Aurora opened her eyes to behold the face of her true love. As Princess

Aurora and Prince Phillip expressed their love to the kingdom, the fairies danced with pleasure—knowing that their beautiful Briar Rose would live happily ever after.

# Disney's

# THE LITTLE MERMAID

## PRINCESS OF THE SEA

Ariel looked lovingly at the man she had rescued. Although her father forbade her to swim to the surface, the adventurous mermaid couldn't help her desire to be a part of the human world. As Prince Eric lay unconscious, she touched his face tenderly. He was so handsome!

She wished with all her heart that she could remain on this beach and dance with this man of her dreams. "What would I give to stay here beside you?" she sang. "What would I do to see you smiling at me?" Somehow, she was determined to find a way!

Sebastian, her

father's trusted friend,

anxiously tried to

persuade Ariel that

she would be happier

under the sea. King

Triton wanted him to

keep an eye on his

youngest daughter, and Sebastian did not want to

disappoint the sea king. "Down here is your home," he told

Ariel, but despite his efforts to make her understand the

wonders of the ocean, nothing could change her wish to be

with Prince Eric. She was in love.

Only Flounder, her best friend, understood. Finding a statue of the prince that had gone down with the shipwreck, he surprised Ariel.

"Flounder, you're the best!" she cried. "It looks just like him."

As she was imagining a romance with Eric, King Triton appeared in Ariel's secret grotto. Seeing

her collection of things from the "barbarian" world above, he raised his trident and destroyed all of Ariel's treasures in a final attempt to protect her from the dangers of the human world.

Upset, Ariel sought the help of the Sea Witch, Ursula. In exchange for the mermaid's voice, Ursula transformed her tail into legs. She would remain human only if she received a kiss of true love before the sun set on the third day.

Happy to be human at last, Ariel wiggled her toes

excitedly while Sebastian watched in shock. "I'm gonna march myself home right now and tell the sea king," he said, but when he looked at the sadness in Ariel's eyes he knew that she would never be happy as a mermaid. "All right," he decided. "I'll help you find your prince."

Scuttle, her
seagull friend,
excitedly arranged
a dress. It wasn't
long before Prince
Eric arrived.

"You're the one!"
he exclaimed. "The
one I have been looking for!" Ariel nodded, but she
couldn't talk. Eric remembered that the girl who had
rescued him had the most beautiful voice. "Oh, you
couldn't be who I thought," he sighed.

Still, he helped her to the castle, and when they ate

dinner together that night, Ariel made him laugh for the

first time in weeks. The next day he took her on a tour of

his kingdom, enchanted by her enthusiasm for everything

from horses to

puppet shows. She

pulled him eagerly

into a dance, and

she was thrilled

when he let her

take the reins on

the ride back to the

castle. Impressed and surprised by her fun-loving nature,

Eric thoroughly enjoyed his new guest.

Sebastian decided to create a romantic mood that

evening as Ariel and Eric rowed together in a quiet

lagoon. With soft music and moonlight on the water, the

prince found himself leaning to kiss Ariel.

Suddenly, Ursula's pet eels tipped the boat!

Hypnotizing Eric, the Sea Witch transformed herself into

the beautiful Vanessa. Pretending to be his mysterious

dream girl, she arranged a wedding to make sure that

Ariel's plan for love would fail.

Scuttle gathered creatures of the ocean to help him stall

the wedding while Flounder pulled Ariel to the ship. As her

friends tugged a magic necklace from Vanessa's neck, Ariel's

voice was restored and the spell on Prince Eric was broken.

He ran to his true love, relieved that she had been the girl he

wanted all along. But their kiss was too late. Ariel had

become a mermaid
once again, and
Ursula pulled her
into the water.

"I lost her once.
I'm not going to lose
her again!" yelled
the Prince as he
dove into the depths of the ocean. Using strength, and the
power of true love, Eric destroyed the powerful Sea Witch.

As he lay exhausted on the shore, Ariel watched him
from afar.

Turning to Sebastian, King Triton asked, "She really does love him, doesn't she?" With tenderness, he granted his beautiful daughter her greatest wish. As Ariel married

her prince, she finally knew true happiness. Sebastian, Flounder, and Scuttle applauded with all of the creatures of the sea as Eric kissed his bride under a rainbow colored with joy.

# DISNEY's

# Beauty and the BEAST

## FRIENDS IN STRANGE PLACES

Long ago, a beautiful young woman was forced to live in an enchanted castle with a hideous beast. Belle had agreed to remain his prisoner in place of her father. Soon she discovered that she and the Beast were

not the only inhabitants.

"This is impossible!" Belle gasped when she realized

that the former servants of the castle had been

transformed into household objects. Mrs. Potts, the

teapot, and her son, Chip, a teacup, quickly put her at ease with their warmhearted welcome. "It'll turn out all right in the end, you'll see," soothed Mrs. Potts.

Meanwhile, the Beast was nervous. The enchantress

who changed him from a handsome prince into an ugly beast had warned him that he must learn to love and be loved before the spell could be broken. He had lost all hope until Belle arrived. Now he was afraid that she would never see him as

anything but a
monster. "She's so
beautiful and I'm . . .
well, look at me!" he
shouted to his
servants.

"You must help
her see past all that,"
Mrs. Potts advised.
She and Lumiere, a
candelabrum, offered
suggestions: act like

a gentleman; compliment her; be gentle and sincere.

"And above all," they said together, "you must control your temper!"

The Beast tried to be polite when he asked Belle to join him for dinner, but he was used to giving orders and

being obeyed. When Belle refused, he burst with anger

and frustration. "If she doesn't eat with me, then she

doesn't eat at all!" he roared.

Despite the master's orders, Mrs. Potts would not let

Belle go hungry. Instead she arranged a fantastic feast as

Lumiere put on a show. The silver and china danced as

he sang, and they

all sang together,

"Be our guest!"

Belle was happy

and laughing.

"That was

wonderful!" she exclaimed, clapping.

Although she was fond of her new friends, Belle wanted nothing to do with the Beast. Only after he proved that he cared, by protecting her from wolves, did she begin to trust him.

Slowly, a friendship developed. One day, as they played in the snow, Belle watched the

Beast feed the birds and realized there was a side of him that she hadn't seen before—a kind and gentle side.

The Beast was happy that Belle was no longer frightened of him. He wanted to give her a gift for bringing happiness back into his life. Covering her eyes, the Beast led her into the enormous library. Belle couldn't believe her eyes when she saw all of the books.

"They're yours,"

the Beast told her. He knew she loved books.

"Thank you so much!" She smiled.

As Belle read to the Beast, their friendship grew stronger. They could talk and laugh with each other as they could with no one else.

Finally, a special evening was planned. The Beast was worried. He wanted everything to be perfect, but he thought he could never be presentable. Cogsworth, the mantel clock, and

Lumiere helped him prepare, assuring him that he looked

handsome and elegant.

When he saw Belle in her ball gown, the Beast bowed

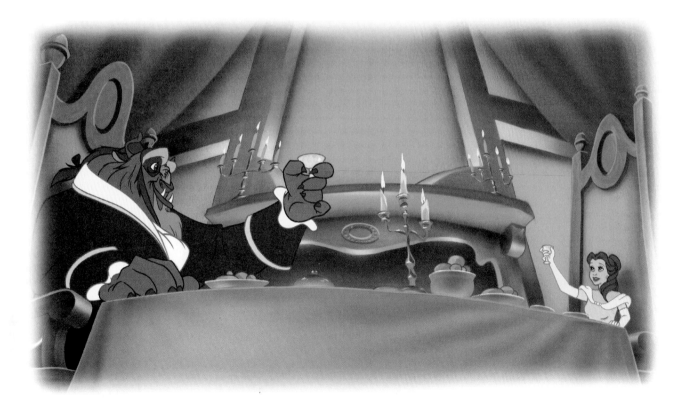

in admiration. At dinner he behaved like a perfect

gentleman and when Mrs. Potts began to sing a love

song, Belle and the Beast were dancing in the ballroom,

happy in each other's arms.

Watching from the doorway, the servants were full of

joy. They could not have guessed that the Beast's love for Belle would send her away. "You are free to go," he told her. Full of compassion, he could not keep her prisoner.

Belle left to visit her father, who was ill. The Beast's heart was broken. As villagers attacked the castle, he let them come. Belle realized that she belonged with the Beast and tried to stop the mob. But she was too late. The Beast lay wounded and dying.

"At least I got to see you one last time," he said, gazing into her eyes.

"No!" she cried. "I love you."

Suddenly, beams of light rained down from the sky. The Beast returned to his human form. In amazement, Belle stared at the handsome prince in front of her.

"Belle, it's me," he assured her.

Looking deep into his eyes, she saw her friend's gentleness and love.

"It is you!" she cried. She kissed him joyfully. Fireworks lit the sky and their friends became human once more. Hugging and laughing they celebrated with a fantastic ball in their shining castle. As they danced, all eyes basked in the timeless love of Beauty and the Beast.

# Disney's

# MULAN

## FRIENDLY ADVICE

Long ago, and far beyond the Great Wall of China, a tiny dragon named Mushu left his ancestral home in search of a young girl, Mulan. Mulan had cut her hair and dressed as a man to take her father's place in the war

against the fierce Huns. Mushu was supposed to protect and guard her.

"Walk like a man. Legs apart," advised Mushu, as she entered camp. "Punch guys in the arm, they like that stuff. Call them names and spit a lot."

Every time Mushu gave her advice, Mulan caused

more trouble. Soon all of the new recruits were fighting. The camp was in total chaos when Captain Shang arrived.

"My name is . . . uh . . . Ping," Mulan told Shang, as she awkwardly tried to sound like a man.

Recently promoted, Shang was wary of possible troublemakers.

Shang was a strong and skillful leader, and although Mulan

felt clumsy and

inadequate, she

worked hard and

used her mind to

finally win his

respect. All of the

soldiers admired

Ping's determination

and they were

inspired by her

actions.  Still, not

even her best friends,

Chien-Po, Ling, and Yao, knew that "Ping" was a woman.

Shang led his troop swiftly to join the Imperial Army.

Mulan and her friends sang songs. Sadly, their good cheer

came to a halt when they discovered that the army and the

village lay in ruins. Shang
was especially upset when
he realized that his father,
the General, had been
killed in battle. As Mulan
tried to comfort him, the
Huns returned.

Proving to be a great
and courageous soldier, Mulan, with Mushu's help,
caused an avalanche that buried the enemy. Wounded in
battle, Mulan was still able to jump on her horse and pull
Shang from the onrushing snow.

As Chien-Po and the others helped them to safety, Shang regained consciousness and looked at Mulan with admiration. "From now on you have my trust," Shang said, thanking her. Mulan's smile soon turned to pain,

and as her wound was treated, they all learned the truth about "Ping."

At this time in China, Mulan's deception was punishable by death, but Shang spared her. "A life for a life," he declared.

Dejected, Mulan watched the troops march away, leaving her alone with Mushu. With a heavy heart Mulan confided in her friend: "I just wanted to do things right, so that when I looked in the mirror I would see someone worthwhile. But I was wrong. I see nothing."

Trying to make her feel better, Mushu confessed that he had set out to

make Mulan a hero so that he would regain his position as guardian. "At least you risked your life to help people you love. I risked your life to help myself," he told her. Mulan embraced the little dragon. How could she be angry with such a friend?

This quiet moment was shattered as Mulan realized that a few of the Huns had survived. Racing to the Imperial City to

warn Shang, Mulan
arrived moments before
the Emperor was taken
prisoner.

Chien-Po, Ling, and
Yao tried unsuccessfully
to break down the palace
door. "Hey, guys, I have
an idea!" Mulan called.
Eager for the help of their
quick-thinking friend,
they let Mulan dress them

as women. Together they scaled the wall and attacked the unsuspecting Huns. Realizing that he could trust her, Shang soon followed her lead.

They rescued the Emperor, but Shan Yu, the Hun leader, angrily attacked Shang. To protect him, Mulan revealed herself as the soldier who had defeated him at the mountain. With ferocity, Shan Yu began to chase her. Putting their heads

together, the girl and the dragon hatched a plan. Leading

Shan Yu to the top of the palace, Mulan grabbed his

sword and pinned his cloak to the roof just as Mushu

shot a rocket toward him. Shan Yu was blasted into a tower of fireworks.

Mulan was happy to leave for home. She realized that she was special enough as herself, and that she had friends she could count on. She presented the Emperor's sword to her father, and he welcomed her back. Shang followed her, realizing, with the Emperor's help, that his feelings for Mulan had grown. She was much more than a good fighter. Finally, Mulan's heart was full.

As for Mushu, the joyful little dragon regained his guardianship. "Send out for eggrolls!" he shouted to the happy Ancestors.

# Disney's

# DUMBO

## If Not for Friends . . .

Dumbo's mother was locked away. Poor little Dumbo felt alone in the world. Without his mother's tender caresses and playful games, he was sad and lonely. The other elephants blamed him for his own mother's imprisonment. They laughed at his big ears and

turned their backs on him when he most needed caring and understanding.

In disbelief, a friendly mouse named Timothy

listened to the mean-spirited gossip of the large elephants. Knowing that they would be terrified of a little mouse like him, he decided to give them the fright of their life. After all, someone had to stick up for little Dumbo. What was wrong with having big ears anyway? thought Timothy.

As far as he was concerned, Dumbo was a cute baby elephant.

So Timothy waved his arms and stuck out his

tongue. The elephants shrieked in fear, climbing poles to get away from the small mouse. "Pick on someone your own size!" yelled Timothy.

He chuckled at their silliness. "Imagine, being afraid of a small mouse," he laughed. "Wait till I tell the little guy." But Dumbo was scared of Timothy, too. He hid himself in

a bale of hay and would not come out even for a peanut.

"I'm your friend," Timothy

assured him. He told Dumbo that his ears were special.

Then he promised to help him get his mother freed if the

little elephant would come out. Hesitantly, Dumbo finally

looked out at his new protector. Deciding to trust

Timothy, they went out

in search of a miracle.

"We'll make you a

star of the circus,"

suggested Timothy

confidently. He came

up with a plan.

Sneaking into the

ringmaster's tent that night, the mouse whispered his great idea to the sleeping man. "Dumbo!" he repeated over and over.

Thinking the idea had come to him in a dream, the ringmaster announced his amazing new act: the smallest

elephant leaping from a springboard to the top of an amazing pyramid of pachyderms!

Dumbo was nervous, but

Timothy encouraged him to try. Running toward the

springboard, the little elephant tripped over his ears and

fell, knocking over the enormous pyramid and collapsing

the tent.

After that, to make matters worse, the ringmaster made

Dumbo a clown.

The poor little

guy didn't trust

the other clowns

to keep him safe.

They forced him

to jump from a

burning building. Dumbo had never been so scared and humiliated! When the show was over, the little elephant was inconsolable.

Timothy tried to comfort his friend. He offered peanuts as he washed the clown paint off with warm, soapy water. Still, Dumbo did not stop crying. Timothy knew that the only one who could help Dumbo now was his mother. So Timothy

arranged for a short visit.

Even though only her trunk could hug him, Dumbo

basked in his mother's love. Although he was sad to go

back to his tent without her, Dumbo was thankful for
Timothy's help.

The next morning, after some strange and restless dreams,
the mouse and the elephant awoke high up in a tree. Some
crows were laughing as the friends fell into a pond.

"Don't listen to those scarecrows," Timothy told
Dumbo, but the elephant was already walking away, head

down. Everyone
was always
laughing at him,
him and his big
ears.  Only

Timothy believed they would do great things.

"That's it, Dumbo!" cried his friend. Timothy had been trying to figure out how they had gotten up in that tree, when suddenly he realized how special Dumbo's ears really were. The perfect wings! "You can fly!" cheered Timothy.

This news made the crows fall over laughing. "Have you ever seen an elephant fly?" they jeered.

Defending his friend, Timothy yelled at the crows for being so insensitive. "How would you like to be taken away from your mother when you were just a baby and then be sent out into a cold, cruel, heartless world?" he ranted.

The crows apologized. They really hadn't meant any harm.

"What he needs is this magic feather," offered one crow.

Timothy showed his friend: "Look, Dumbo, you can fly!"

Holding the feather in his trunk, Dumbo closed his eyes and flapped his ears.  He wanted so much to believe

Timothy! He was flying!

When he opened his eyes again the little elephant was overjoyed. He held the feather tightly, flying through the sky like a bird. Timothy cheered from his seat on

Dumbo's hat while the crows praised the elephant's talent.

It was not long before Timothy's prediction of stardom was a reality. As Dumbo jumped from the burning building again he dropped the magic feather and panicked, but Timothy quickly assured him that he could fly on his own. Restoring his confidence allowed Dumbo to soar, astonishing everyone

who had once made fun of the elephant's big ears.

Finally, Dumbo and his mother were reunited! With love and pride, Timothy signed on as manager for the world's only flying elephant.

# Disney's

# The Fox and the Hound

## FRIENDS FOREVER

Tod was a fox and Copper was a hound. They played hide-and-seek, they swam in the water, and they wrestled and ran together. Since they were unaware that a fox and a hound were not supposed to play together, a

friendship
developed. Each
morning they
looked forward to
meeting in the
woods for another
day of carefree fun.

"We'll always be
friends, right,
Copper?" Tod
asked one day as they splashed in the pond.

Copper agreed. They were best friends. Neither could

think of a reason why that should change as they chased each other in the afternoon light.

Then one morning, Tod was disappointed when Copper did not come to play. Amos, the puppy's master,

had decided that it was time for Copper to learn to hunt, like his old dog, Chief. Copper loved Chief like a father. He was eager to impress him and soon learned how to track the scents

of many animals, including foxes.

While Copper was away, Tod was lonely. Mrs. Tweed, who had cared for Tod since he was orphaned as a cub, kept him company during the long winter. Still, the growing fox missed his friends. He missed Big Mama, the owl, with her exciting stories and wise advice. He missed the silly antics of his bird friends, Dinky and Boomer, as they tried unsuccessfully to capture a caterpillar. Most of all, he missed playing with his friend Copper.

When spring finally came, he raced outside, overjoyed to be outdoors. As he talked excitedly to Big Mama, Dinky, and Boomer, he heard Amos Slade's truck coming

down the road. Copper was home!

His friends tried to warn Tod that Copper would be different now that the hound was a hunting dog, but Tod refused to believe that Copper would ever become his enemy. "Copper's my friend!" he insisted.

That night, while Chief and Amos slept, Tod paid a visit to his old pal. He was surprised when Copper said, "We can't play together anymore." As the fox tried to convince his friend to reconsider, Chief woke up and raced after Tod.

When Amos

ordered Copper to help

track the fox, the

hound dog purposely

led the hunter and

Chief in the wrong

direction. "I don't want

to see you get hurt," Copper whispered to the scared fox.

"Run that way." Tod obeyed happily, realizing that their

friendship wasn't over yet.

When the fox returned home, Mrs. Tweed was very

anxious.  She wanted to keep Tod safe and happy, but knew

that she could no longer protect him from Amos. Sadly, she hugged the fox, removed his collar, and left him in a wildlife sanctuary where she thought he would be safe.

The first night was long and difficult. Tod was scared and confused. He missed his warm home and his friends.

Beginning to despair, he caught sight of the most beautiful creature he had ever seen! It was Vixey, whom Big Mama had called upon to help the lonely fox. She batted her lovely eyelashes with a sweet "Hello," and Tod was in love.

Happily, the two foxes roamed the wilderness together. Vixey soon taught Tod how to fish and how to get along in his new forest home. Big Mama, Dinky, and Boomer even came to

visit, and Tod knew that everything would be all right.

That evening, as he and Vixey were returning to their den, Tod spied a shiny object in the leaves. *Snap! Snap!*

*Snap!* went the traps that Amos had set. Although hunting wasn't allowed in the sanctuary, Amos and Copper were after Tod. They blamed him for injuries that Chief had suffered when the hounds had last chased Tod.

With speed and courage, Tod and Vixey escaped Amos and Copper, but watched desperately as the hunters were attacked by a grizzly bear. Tod couldn't let his old friend

come to harm, so he risked his own life to lead the bear over a waterfall. As Tod climbed onto the bank breathlessly, Amos pointed his rifle at the fox.

"If he wants to kill you, he'll have to shoot me first,"

said Copper as he stepped in front of his old friend.

Copper knew that Tod had risked his own life to save

him and his master and he finally realized how important

friendship was. A true friend, like Tod, would be a

friend forever.

In peace and contentment, Tod and Vixey remained together, their love blossoming in the freedom of their forest home. Occasionally Tod would look upon Copper from a cliff above the valley, knowing that even time, distance, and the laws of nature could not break the bond between them.

# FOR THE LOVE OF A PRINCESS

Princess Dot believed in Flik even when his inventions caused trouble. After all, he was smart and kind and a good listener. Although Dot was only a small ant, Flik treated her as if she were important. "Someday you'll be big," he told the little princess.

Showing her a rock, he told her to pretend it was a seed. "It's very small now,

but when it grows it will be a great tree."

When Flik decided to go to the city, Dot stood by his side. He was in search of rough bugs that could fight the grasshoppers who were terrorizing the ant colony. The other ants did not think that Flik would make it back alive. Still, Dot waved confidently to her friend as he sailed away on a dandelion puff.

"He'll bring back the biggest, meanest, roughest bugs you've ever seen!" she told two skeptical boy ants.

Soon Flik did return. "You did it!" Dot cheered happily, but her sister, Princess Atta, was worried. Could these big bugs really conquer the grasshoppers? No one knew that Flik had brought back a troupe of circus

performers who had assumed Flik was a talent scout.

Atta was won over when the strange group bravely

rescued Dot from a dangerous bird. "Hooray!" shouted

the ants. Their applause stunned the circus bugs. No one

had ever appreciated them before. They were filled with

pride as the colony gave them the heroes' treatment.

When the young blueberry scouts asked for autographs,

the circus troupe decided to stay awhile, but they made it

clear to Flik that they were not fighters. He assured them

that with his new plan to build a bird, they would not

have to fight. Then he promised to help them escape when

the grasshoppers arrived.

After Dot's rescue, Princess Atta pulled Flik aside. "I want to apologize," she told him, explaining her doubts about the warriors. "I guess I was afraid of making a mistake. No one believes that I will be a good queen. It's as if they're all just waiting for me . . ."

" . . . to fail," Flik interrupted. "I know the feeling."

Princess Atta knew that Flik did understand, and she felt guilty for not believing in him. Things would be different now, she thought. She was proud to be a part of Flik's new plan, and she directed the colony to follow his orders as they all built a bird to chase Hopper and his bully followers away for good.

When the bird was finished, Flik told the circus bugs they could leave, but they had changed their minds. They believed in Flik. "Dim don't want to go," stated the giant

blue bug, and the others agreed.

It was at that moment that the ants discovered that they had put their faith in circus performers, not warriors. Atta couldn't believe that Flik had lied to her! She had trusted him! Now she angrily sent him away with his circus pals.

"It's okay." The circus bugs comforted the forlorn Flik. "Being a circus performer's not such a bad life."

But Flik was too unhappy to be cheered up.  When Dot caught up with them, Flik was still feeling worthless, but the little princess knew his heart was true. She and the circus bugs believed that his plan would work if only they could convince Flik to trust in himself again.

Dot knew how. She placed a stone by his side, reminding him of their old conversation about a little

seed becoming a big tree. Nodding gratefully to his remarkable friend, Flik returned to Ant Island with Dot and the circus bugs.

Flik worked valiantly with the help of his friends, but their project went awry, and Hopper was angrier than ever. When Flik bravely stood up to the bully

grasshopper, Princess Atta realized that she had judged

Flik harshly. Finally she saw what Dot had known all

along. Flik had always put the colony's interests first.

When Hopper took Flik hostage, Princess Atta knew

she was his only chance. Risking her own life, she flew

after them, grabbing Flik away from the grasshopper. As

Flik advised her to fly toward a bird's nest, she trusted his

wise instinct, and Hopper soon became lunch for three

hungry hatchlings. At last, the ants were free!

Happily, Atta and Flik returned to Ant Island. Flik was proud to see Atta crowned Queen, and she happily appointed him the colony's official inventor.

Only the circus bugs felt a tinge of sadness. They knew

it was time to move on. Still, their hearts were full of new joy and confidence. Gratefully, they waved good-bye to Princess Dot, Flik, and Queen Atta.

# Walt Disney's

# _Lady_ and the TRAMP

## OPPOSITES ATTRACT

"It's a beautiful night," Tony sang as Lady and the Tramp ate the best spaghetti in town. Watching the musicians, the two dogs didn't realize that they were eating the same strand of spaghetti until their noses met.

Bashfully, Lady looked away, but Tramp gently pushed a meatball toward his beautiful companion. What a romantic night, they both thought as they walked around town with their stomachs full and the stars smiling down on the quiet streets.

With unspoken commitment they placed their paws side by side in wet cement, gazing at each other lovingly. Then Tramp guided

Lady through a peaceful park and they fell asleep. When Lady awoke at dawn she was happy, but startled to realize that she had been away from home for so long.

Tramp was surprised that Lady wanted to return to her fenced yard. "Open your eyes to what a dog's life can really be," he told her as they gazed at a beautiful view of the country. "Who knows what wonderful experiences two dogs can have, and it's all ours for the taking."

Lady smiled. "It sounds wonderful," she agreed. "But who'll watch over the baby?"

Tramp realized that Lady was very loyal to her human

family. Jim Dear and Darling were very kind, giving her the best food, a warm home, and lots of love. "With Lady here I think life is quite complete," Jim Dear had once said, and now that the baby had been born their lives were even more full. Lady felt needed in a way that she had never known before. She was anxious to get home in

order to protect the little one who had become very dear to her heart.

However, when she returned, Jim Dear and Darling were still on their trip. Aunt Sarah, angry at Lady for running away, chained the poor dog to her doghouse.

Misunderstood by the old woman, Lady was treated harshly, but thankfully Aunt Sarah did not attempt to put another muzzle on her.

With a heavy heart Lady resigned herself to a cold and lonely night, but no sooner had she settled down than she was startled awake. A large rat was sneaking into the yard!

Yanked roughly by her chain when she tried to give chase,

Lady watched helplessly as the rat scurried through an

open window to

the baby's room.

Fearfully, she

barked with all

her might.

   "What's wrong,

Pidge?" called

Tramp, running to

help. When Lady

explained, he

hurried to protect the baby and fought with the vicious rat until the creature was dead. Lady, who had tugged herself free, stood proudly by his side as Aunt Sarah entered to check on the crying baby.

"Merciful heavens!" Aunt Sarah exclaimed when she saw the crib overturned and the room in disarray.  Not

seeing the rat, she blamed the two dogs and called the

dogcatcher to take Tramp away. Lady barked desperately.

Luckily, Jim Dear and Darling soon arrived home.

"She's trying to tell us something," Jim Dear insisted.

Quickly, Lady led them to the rat.

Overhearing the humans, Lady's friends Jock and Trusty realized what had happened. "We've got to stop that wagon!" declared Trusty, chasing after the

dogcatcher. Jock followed and they soon tracked Tramp

down. However, when they attempted to make the

dogcatcher stop, the wagon veered out of control and

turned on its side, toppling onto poor old Trusty. Jock

was inconsolable until he discovered Trusty had only broken a leg.

Just then, Jim Dear and Darling arrived with Lady.

Surprised, Tramp returned home with his new family,

realizing that some humans could be trusted after all.

Living in a fenced yard wasn't so bad, thought Tramp as

he proudly showed Jock and Trusty his new collar and

license. Even the baby was happy playing with the new puppies. Lady stood watch over her human family and her canine family with joy in her heart.

# Disney's

# The Rescuers

## SMALL MICE, BIG HEARTS

Tears slid down Penny's cheeks as she looked over the swamp. "Have faith," Rufus had told her at the orphanage. The old cat believed that Penny was extra special. He was sure that a mother and father were

looking for a girl just like her. But how would they ever find her in Devil's Bayou? She had tried to escape many

times, but Medusa's pet crocodiles kept finding her and bringing her back to the creepy riverboat.

Watching Penny from a tiny leaf-boat below, two small mice

wondered if they could help the poor child. So far they had been tossed from a car, nearly drowned, chased by crocodiles, and shot at by Medusa.

"The Rescue Aid Society is depending on us," Bianca reminded her friend. Bernard nodded. He was only a janitor at the society, but no mouse was more loyal. When the beautiful Miss Bianca had chosen him to be her

coagent, he couldn't have been prouder.

So as Penny prayed for help, the mice climbed through her window. "Don't worry, Teddy. We'll be all right!" Penny sobbed.

"Penny," Bianca called softly. As the child raised her

tear-stained face, the mice explained that they had found her message in a bottle and had come to rescue her.

Penny's eyes lit up. She twirled Teddy in the air excitedly. Then she stopped short. "Didn't you bring anyone big with you? Like the police?"

Bernard shook his head honestly.

"But if the three of us work together and have a little faith . . ." Bianca started to say.

"Things will turn out right," Penny finished. Smiling, she thought of Rufus. Perhaps these mice could help.

Together they came up with a plan. First Bernard sent

for help from their friends who lived in the Bayou. Penny

showed them an old elevator that would make a good

cage for the crocodiles. They could light fireworks to

distract Medusa and get away on the swamp boat. "This is so exciting!" Bianca declared, hugging the bashful Bernard. Even Penny laughed for the first time in weeks.

However, their fun did not last long. Bernard and Bianca hid in Penny's dress pocket when Medusa came to get the poor girl. Once again Penny would be forced to look for the Devil's Eye diamond.

"Teddy doesn't like

it down there!" pleaded the little girl. She was afraid of the dark cave, but Medusa didn't care. She grabbed the teddy bear. "You'll find that diamond or you'll never see your precious Teddy again!"

Frightened, Penny obeyed. The cave was spooky but at least Bernard and Bianca were there to help her this time. Suddenly the ground shook and they looked toward the gaping hole where water hissed and gurgled dangerously. "If I were a pirate that's just where I'd hide the Devil's Eye," said Bernard.

Although it was dangerous to get to the other side, the

mice helped each other across the hole. Sure enough, the diamond was in there, hidden inside a skull! Bianca and Bernard tried to

pull it free, but the diamond was too big. "It's stuck tight!" Penny yelled to Medusa. The tide was coming in fast, but Medusa would not pull her to safety. "You'll bring me that diamond or you'll never see daylight again!" she roared.

Bravely, Penny crossed the hole and pried the skull open with a sword just as the water rushed in. Caught in a whirlpool, Bernard and Bianca cried for help. As Penny risked

her life to save her friends, a wave tossed them upward and

dumped them into the bucket just in time.

"Give me back my Teddy!" cried Penny, but Medusa

ignored her desperate pleas. Hiding the diamond in his

stuffing, Medusa held Penny at bay with her gun.

Luckily, Bernard and Bianca thought quickly. They tied a

wire across the doorway, causing Medusa to trip. As

Penny snatched Teddy, the Rescuers ran after her and

climbed aboard the swamp boat.

"We did it!" cheered Bernard when they were safe.

Bernard and Bianca watched Penny on television the

next day. They were glad to see their friend so happy.

Penny had been adopted and stood lovingly with Teddy

and her new parents. "Two little mice rescued me," she told the world. Never would Penny forget her courageous friends!

# Walt Disney's

# Bambi

## TWITTERPATED

As Prince Bambi learned to walk, an outspoken young rabbit became his cheerful guide in the outdoor world. Clumsily, Bambi stumbled after Thumper and his brothers and sisters. "He's a little wobbly, isn't

he?" asked Thumper, and the bunnies all giggled as the little prince got used to his thin, young legs.

As they explored, Bambi stopped to look at some

beautifully colored birds. "Say *bird*," Thumper prompted. "Burr . . ." tried the little fawn. "Bir-duh!"

Thumper corrected. Soon Bambi was saying his first word as the bunnies happily cheered him on.

*Butterfly* and then *flower* were the next words Bambi learned. Thumper showed him how to smell the fragrant

blooms, but when Bambi leaned into the flowers he touched a small black nose. "Flower!" the fawn pronounced proudly. Thumper rolled over laughing as he saw a skunk lift his head from the blossoms. "He's not a flower," Thumper began to explain. "He's a little . . ."

"That's all right," interrupted the bashful skunk. "He can call me Flower if he wants to." Happy with his new name, Flower held a special place in his heart for the

young prince.

Soon after, while playing in the meadow, the little deer

captured another heart. When he was looking at his

reflection in the water,

the pretty face of a

female fawn, Faline,

appeared beside his

own. In shock, Bambi

jumped backward.

Suddenly he was shy as

he looked into the other

fawn's big blue eyes.

Faline laughed heartily at Bambi's nervousness.

Bounding toward him, she caused him to stumble through some reeds and land with a splash in the creek. Mischievously, the doe teased her playmate by leaning through the reeds to kiss him, then running around to lick his other cheek.

Bambi was not nearly as amused as his tormentor.

"You!" he yelled, pouncing at Faline. She giggled and ran and he chased her through the meadow, his anger changing quickly to enjoyment. It was fun to have another deer to play with.

Quickly, the seasons changed. Bambi woke one morning and he was amazed to see the world covered in white. "It's snow," his mother explained. "Winter has come."

Indeed it had! Bambi and Thumper reveled in the winter wonderland. Thumper even tried to teach his friend to ice skate, but hooves and long, thin legs are not meant for slippery surfaces. Thumper patiently pushed,

pulled, and prodded to keep Bambi upright. Flower,

however, did not share in their merriment. "All of us

flowers sleep in the winter," he informed the others.

As the seasons passed, Bambi and his friends became

handsome young males. Friend Owl warned them that

they would soon find themselves "twitterpated"—falling in love.

"It won't happen to me!" each of the three friends declared. Haughtily, they walked away.

Then, without warning, Flower felt his heart pumping.

Two of the prettiest blue eyes he had ever seen were staring at him through a garden of daisies. As the female skunk kissed him, Flower turned red all over. Smiling, he followed her through the blossoms, turning only once to

give Bambi and Thumper a helpless shrug.

"Twitterpated!" cried Thumper. He listened to the happy giggles as Flower bounded after the lovely female skunk. In disbelief, he and Bambi continued down the path.

Suddenly, Thumper stopped in his tracks! He turned to look at a gorgeous bunny fluffing the fur on her cheeks. With a flutter of long eyelashes and a kiss, Thumper's foot began thumping wildly. Owl was right.

He had fallen in love.

Now Bambi was

alone. As he stopped

for a drink at the

creek, he saw Faline.

She had grown into a

beautiful doe. Bambi

startled at her

reflection and backed

into a blossoming

tree, catching his antlers in the branches. "Hello, Bambi."

She laughed gently. "Remember me?"

This time she wasn't teasing as she leaned to kiss him, and he wasn't rubbing the kiss away as he had when they were fawns. Instead, his eyes grew big and round. He bounded after Faline as if in a dream filled with clouds.

As they pranced through the meadow, Bambi was so happy he felt as if he was flying.

Deciding to spend their lives together, Bambi and Faline soon became proud parents of a pair of fawns. All of the animals in the forest came to gaze at Bambi's children. Thumper brought his large family. Even Flower had a little baby skunk to hurry along. How happy Bambi was to have everyone he loved

share his joy!

# Walt Disney's

# Snow White
## and the Seven Dwarfs

## FRIENDS TO COUNT ON

Snow White glanced around her. It was very peaceful in the thicket and the sun was shining in the blue sky. It had looked different at night. She had been so afraid!

"What do you do when things go wrong?" Snow White asked the woodland animals who had come to gaze at the lovely princess.

As the birds began to sing she joined them. Singing always made her feel better. Then she asked the animals if they knew of a place where she might stay. They led Snow White to a clearing where she noticed a charming little cottage.

When Snow White entered there was no one home. The room was dirty with dishes piled high in the sink and clothes tossed about. As she counted the adorable little chairs at the table, Snow White thought seven untidy children must live in this cottage.

Perhaps they have no mother, she thought sadly.

Deciding to surprise them by cleaning and making dinner, Snow White sang a cheerful song as she worked. The squirrels, chipmunks, deer, raccoons, and birds helped

her dust, wash, and sweep. Snow White put soup on to cook, then climbed upstairs where she discovered seven little beds. Names were carved into

each one: Doc, Happy, Sneezy, Dopey, Grumpy, Bashful, and Sleepy. What strange names for children, she thought, but the beds looked wonderfully inviting and she was awfully tired. As she lay across three of the small

mattresses, the birds covered her tenderly with a blanket, and Snow White fell fast asleep.

Soon seven dwarfs came home. "The whole house is clean!"

Doc

exclaimed.

Nervously

they tiptoed

upstairs.

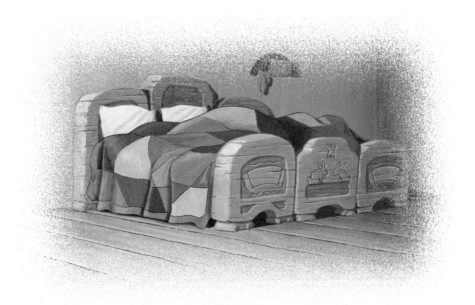

Seeing a large

form under the sheets, they assumed it was a monster and

got ready to attack as Snow White began to stir.

Surprised, they stared at the beautiful girl. "An angel,"

whispered Bashful, but Grumpy thought differently. "All

females are poison!" he insisted.

The nervous dwarfs hid behind the bed. The Princess

was startled as they peeked at her over the footboards. "Oh, you're little men!" she cried happily. Smiling, she guessed their names and explained how she had been sent away by her stepmother, the Queen. "She tried to kill me," Snow White told them, but Grumpy was unsympathetic.

"Send her away!" he yelled, nervous about the evil queen's black magic.

"She won't find me here," the Princess promised, "and I'll wash, and keep house, and cook . . ."

The dwarfs thought of the apple dumplings and gooseberry pies that Snow White could make. "She stays!" they agreed. Happily they followed

her downstairs as she went to check on the soup.

"Wash up or you'll not get a bite to eat!" said Snow White as she checked their dirty hands. Although the dwarfs dreaded soap and water, they wanted to make the Princess happy.

After dinner they played music and danced. Even

Grumpy played the pipe
organ. Never had they
had so much fun or
laughed so hard!

"Now you do
something," they urged
Snow White. She began
to tell them a story about
a princess who fell in
love. "Was it you?" they
asked, and she nodded,
remembering the

charming prince who had appeared as she was singing at

a wishing well. Startled, Snow White had run into the

castle, but when the Prince serenaded her, she looked out

on the balcony. "He was so romantic," she told her new

friends. She had sent him a kiss on the wings of a dove.

Sighing dreamily, the dwarfs gave Snow White their cozy beds for the night. Even Grumpy was happy that she had stayed.

"I'm warnin' ya . . . don't let nobody or nothin' in the house!" he said the next morning as he left for work.

"Why, Grumpy, you do care!" Snow White smiled as Grumpy stomped away. Then she kissed Dopey tenderly and sent him on his way.

Forgetting Grumpy's warning, Snow White allowed a poor old woman into the house that afternoon. The old woman offered her an apple, and not suspecting that it

was the Queen in disguise, the poor girl took one bite of the poisoned apple and fell to the floor.

Sadly, the dwarfs and forest animals grieved for their beloved princess until the day a prince appeared, having heard the story of a lovely girl in a glass coffin.

Recognizing her as the Princess he'd been searching for, he kissed her.

Slowly, Snow White awakened. The happy prince

lifted her in his arms as the dwarfs and animals rejoiced around them. Cheerfully giving each of her friends a good-bye kiss, Snow White turned to her true love. As the birds sang, the happy couple walked toward a golden castle, where they lived happily ever after.

# DISNEY's

# Aladdin

## THE PRINCESS
## WHO DIDN'T WANT TO MARRY

Princess Jasmine giggled with her friend Rajah. Although Rajah was a tiger he had always been her closest friend. Now he held a piece of Prince Achmed's pants in his mouth. He and Jasmine were both glad to be rid of the selfish suitor.

Jasmine's father, however, was not amused. "The law says you must be married to a prince by your next birthday."

Jasmine thought the law was unfair. She wanted to

marry for love. "Try to understand, I've never done a thing on my own," she explained. Lately she wished that she were not a princess at all. She felt as trapped as the caged doves.

That night the princess disguised herself, planning

to escape. As she began to climb over the palace wall, Rajah tugged on her dress. He was sad to see Jasmine leave, but knew what was best for her. "I can't stay here and have my life lived for me," she explained sorrowfully.

In the marketplace, life was busy and exciting. With compassion,

Jasmine handed an apple to a poor child. However, when she was unable to pay, the vendor grabbed her angrily. Luckily, a handsome stranger came to her rescue. Running swiftly, they escaped to his rooftop home.

Jasmine was thrilled with the thought of such freedom. This young man had no one to tell him what he could or couldn't do. As she was imagining his carefree life, the man looked longingly toward the palace. It would be

wonderful to live there, he thought, without having to worry about where to find his next meal.

"Sometimes I just feel so trapped," they both expressed at the same time.

Surprised, they looked at each other. Feeling a deep bond with this handsome stranger, Jasmine leaned to kiss

him, when suddenly guards burst upon them. There was nowhere to escape.

"Do you trust me?" asked the young man, holding out his hand to her. She looked into his brown eyes and placed her fingers in his grip. Quickly, they jumped off the tall building, their fall broken by a pile of hay. "I've got you

this time, Street Rat!"
yelled another guard.
Jasmine revealed herself
as a princess but they still
arrested her friend. "My
orders come from Jafar,"
the guard told her.

Back at the palace,
Jasmine confronted her
father's chief advisor. The
evil Jafar cruelly deceived
her into thinking that her

handsome stranger was dead. "Oh, Rajah," she wept, as the tiger tried to comfort her.

Many days later, on the streets of Agrabah, there was a magnificent parade. Princess Jasmine, still grieving,

watched from her balcony. Trumpets were blaring, animals were doing tricks, fireworks blasted, but most impressive was Prince Ali, sitting on top of an enormous elephant, throwing gold coins into the crowd. Jasmine shook her head in disgust. Did he think he could buy her hand in marriage?

With anger, she yelled at the prince, "I am not a prize to be won!" But Prince Ali would not give up. That evening he appeared on her balcony. Rajah growled

protectively and was about to chase him away but

Jasmine thought he looked familiar. She stepped closer

and he showed her his magic carpet. "We could get out of

the palace . . . see

the world," Prince

Ali offered.

Jasmine

hesitated until he

leaned forward

offering his hand.

"Do you trust

me?" he asked, and immediately Jasmine knew this was the same stranger she had met in the marketplace. Eagerly she climbed aboard and the carpet took them into the star-filled sky. Never had she seen such wonders! As they flew, she felt happier than she ever had before. Leaning on Prince Ali's shoulder she held his hand, not wanting the romantic night to end.

Unfortunately, Jafar soon discovered Prince Ali's magic lamp. He revealed Jasmine's love to be Aladdin, a poor boy from Agrabah. He had used a wish from the

genie in the lamp to transform himself into Prince Ali.

"Jasmine, I'm sorry I lied to you about being a prince," said Aladdin humbly. Jasmine held his

hands. She didn't love him for being a prince. She loved him for himself. Even the Sultan realized that Aladdin was worthy. When her father changed the law to allow his daughter to marry the man of her choice, Jasmine said, "I choose Aladdin." As fireworks lit the sky and the Genie and Abu waved good-bye, Aladdin and Jasmine shared a kiss on their magic carpet. Beneath them was a whole new world where they would live together, happily ever after.

# DISNEP's
# POCAHONTAS

## LISTEN TO YOUR HEART

Pocahontas looked into the wise face of her ancient friend, Grandmother Willow. Troubled by a dream about a spinning arrow, she wondered, "What is my path?" Grandmother Willow told her there were spirits in

the earth, water, and sky. "If you listen they will guide you," she advised. Climbing to the top of the leafy branches, Pocahontas felt the wind around her and saw strange white clouds in the distance.

The clouds were sails of a ship that carried strangers to the land. Pocahontas secretly watched an adventurous man exploring the forest that afternoon. She was drawn toward him,

following in his footsteps until suddenly he jumped out of the shadows. The two stared at each other for many moments. John Smith had never seen a woman so beautiful and mysterious. He wanted to get closer, but his movement scared Pocahontas, who ran like a deer, away to the river where she kept her canoe.

"Wait," he called as he ran after her. "I'm not going to hurt you." Although he spoke a different language, she listened with her heart.

"I'm Pocahontas," she told him as she took his outstretched hand. Together they talked and bonded in a way that Pocahontas had never experienced before. They laughed at Meeko, a mischievous raccoon, who rummaged for biscuits in John's bag. Pocahontas quieted Flit, her hummingbird

friend, who flew in John's face, protecting her.

Pocahontas knew in her heart the goodness inside of

John Smith, and realized she was safe.

Pocahontas began to sing, guiding him through the forest. "We are all connected to each other," she told him. She showed him the gentleness of a mother bear with her cubs. They listened to the wolves cry and watched eagles fly to the top of a sycamore tree. "How tall does a

sycamore grow?" asked Pocahontas. "You'll never know if you cut it down."

As nature touched his soul, John Smith began to

realize that his people had much to learn. With

Pocahontas as his teacher, he could hear the voices in the

mountains and even see colors in the wind. This amazing

young woman was right. No one owned the land.

Understanding, he held her hands and gazed into her brown eyes.

Back at the Indian village, Nakoma was worried about her childhood friend. She had been warned that the settlers were dangerous, yet when John Smith appeared in the cornfield Pocahontas made her promise not to tell anyone. Nakoma kept her silence but felt uncomfortable as she watched the two figures

disappear into the evening shadows.

Pocahontas led John to Grandmother Willow while

Meeko and Flit chased after their new playmate, Percy, a dog

from the settler's camp. The ancient eyes looked kindly into

John's blue ones. "He has a good soul," she told Pocahontas,

"and he's

handsome, too."

John Smith

laughed. "Oh, I

like her," he said.

Pocahontas was

very happy. When

John Smith left, Grandmother Willow suggested that

perhaps she had found her path.

Nakoma disagreed. She pleaded with Pocahontas not

to see John Smith again, but her friend vanished into the

woods anyway. In fear, Nakoma sent a warrior to look for the Princess. When they returned, John Smith had been taken prisoner and Pocahontas fell to her knees with grief. "I'm sorry," said Nakoma, taking her hands. "I

thought I was doing the right thing."

In the prisoner's tepee, Pocahontas cried. "I'd rather die tomorrow than live a hundred years without knowing you," John Smith told her tenderly.

Pocahontas went to see Grandmother Willow. She wanted to do something, but how could one girl stop a war between two peoples? "I feel so lost," she told the tree spirit. Meeko's ears perked up. Quickly the little raccoon found a compass he had taken from John Smith,

hoping that it would help Pocahontas find her way. Inside was a spinning arrow. "My dream!" exclaimed the young woman.

She knew what her path was as she courageously addressed the fighting villages. Protecting John Smith with her own body she proved that love is stronger than hatred. Although peace ensued, John Smith had already been wounded.

Heavy-hearted,
Pocahontas knew that
he would have to
return to London if
he was to survive. "I'll
always be with you,"
she told him, and she
kissed him good-bye.
As she watched his
ship sail away, the
wind touched them
both once again.

# Disney's

# THE LION KING

## FRIENDSHIP MEANS NO WORRIES

Simba carried a heavy burden for a young lion cub. Timon, a meerkat, and Pumbaa, a warthog, wanted to help their troubled friend.

"You've gotta put the past behind you," Timon advised him. "Repeat after me . . . Hakuna Matata!"

This was Timon and Pumbaa's philosophy. "It means no worries," they sang, and soon Simba had joined the group.

With Pumbaa and Timon as his playmates, Simba learned to laugh again. He learned to live in the moment. The trio feasted on bugs, swam in the river, sang songs, told jokes,

and slept under the stars.

Life was good as long as Simba didn't think about painful memories—his father's death, and his uncle Scar saying that Simba was responsible. Scar had told him to run away and Simba was still running, running from guilt and pain.

One afternoon Simba's childhood playmate, Nala, came hunting. The lioness had no idea that her friend was

still alive. She was searching for food and had chosen Pumbaa as her target.

"She's gonna eat me!" cried the panicked warthog, who was stuck under a tree root. Just in time, Simba jumped to the rescue. Only after Nala had pinned him on the ground did he recognize the trick she had always used when they were young.

"Nala!" he cried joyfully. Thrilled that Simba was alive, the lioness pranced around him in disbelief.

"This is Nala. She's my best friend," Simba said, introducing Timon and Pumbaa. The two lions had been playmates, always conspiring to escape the watchful eye of Zazu, his father's advisor. Even when Simba had led

her to the dangerous elephant graveyard, Nala stuck by his side. "I thought you were very brave," she had whispered as they were led home. Simba was glad to see her again.

"You don't know how much this will mean to everyone . . . what it means to me," Nala told him. "I've really missed you."

Simba nuzzled her. "I've missed you, too,"

he said, but he was still not ready to face his past.

Together the lions walked in the magic evening air. They chased each other through the grass and tumbled down a hill. As they landed softly, Nala kissed Simba. It was a wonderful tender moment and the two embraced.

"Why didn't you come back?" Nala eventually asked. Simba had been waiting for this question and hung his head in shame. "No one needs me," he responded, but Nala disagreed. She told him that Scar had let the hyenas destroy the Pride Lands. "If you don't do something soon, everyone will starve," she told him. "You're our only hope."

Still, Simba was not ready to return. He walked guiltily away. "You can't change the past," he said to himself, "and it's all my fault."

Close by, the wise baboon Rafiki called out to him. "You're Mufasa's boy," he reminded Simba. Then he

led the lion to a pool of water and told him to look hard at his reflection. "He lives in you!" the baboon told him.

Suddenly the clouds changed shape and Simba saw his

father. "Remember who you are," Mufasa said from the stars. "You are my son and the one true king."

Simba was afraid of what he knew he must do. Knocking some sense into his friend, Rafiki struck the lion with his stick. Simba was surprised.

"Why did you do that?"

"It doesn't matter. It's in the past," Rafiki told him.

"The past can hurt. You can either run from it or learn from it." As Rafiki swung his stick again, Simba ducked, avoiding the blow. Understanding the lesson, he returned to the Pride Lands to challenge his uncle.

Sadly, he looked at the destruction Scar had caused. "If I don't fight for it, who will?" he wondered.

"I will," Nala answered, joining him proudly. Timon and Pumbaa had followed as well. "Simba, if it's important to you, we're with you to the end," they told him.

The three followed Simba to Pride Rock. Everyone

fought in the battle, even old Rafiki. The lionesses chased

the hyenas away while
Simba took care of Scar.

"I killed Mufasa,"
admitted his evil uncle.
Anger surged through
Simba: anger for the
death of his father, anger
for years of guilt, anger
for the destruction of his
home. Using the trick
that Nala taught him, he
flipped Scar over a cliff.

With a great roar, Simba finally claimed his rightful place as king. The lionesses echoed his proclamation and happily welcomed him home. As news of Simba's return spread, animals once again roamed free. The land began

to heal, and Simba and Nala started a family of their own.

# Disney's

# ROBIN hOOD

## PRINCE OF OUTLAWS

Long ago in Sherwood Forest there lived two outlaws. Their names were Robin Hood and Little John. They were smart and fast and the best archers in the land. Prince John wanted them arrested and sent a posse after them, but they escaped. With their many disguises and skills

they stole his gold, jewels, and once, even his royal robe. The folks in Nottingham thought of the outlaws as heroes. When the Sheriff came to collect high taxes, Robin never failed to replenish the coins in the villagers' pockets. Once the Sheriff even took a bunny's birthday money, leaving the large rabbit family penniless. When Robin Hood arrived, disguised as a blind beggar, he gave little Skippy his bow and arrow and his hat to make up for the lost present. The bunnies were delighted and Mother Rabbit thanked him as he put a bag of gold in her hand.

"You risk so much to keep our hopes alive . . . bless you!" she called after him.

As Robin returned to his hideout, the beautiful Maid Marian was dreaming of her childhood sweetheart. Staring at Robin Hood's "wanted" poster, she confided in her best friend, Lady Kluck. "Surely he must know how much I still love him," she sighed. With a smile Klucky assured her that they would be together soon.

Meanwhile, Robin was thinking of Maid Marian as well. "I love her, Johnny," he confessed. Little John was not surprised. "Just marry the girl," he advised, but Robin shook his head hopelessly. "What have I got to offer her?" he asked. "I'm an outlaw. What kind of a future is that?"

Just then Friar Tuck appeared. Overhearing the conversation, he became indignant. "Oh, for heaven's

sake, son!" he exclaimed. "You're no outlaw. Someday you'll be called a great hero!"

Robin Hood and Little John laughed at the thought as Friar Tuck told them about an archery tournament. Maid Marian had promised a kiss to the winner. Robin's eyes gleamed. He could win the contest blindfolded!

In his greatest disguise yet, Robin entered the tournament with a wink at his love. "I wish you luck,"

Maid Marian told him. Then she whispered, "With all my heart."

Unknowingly, Robin had fallen right into a trap set by Prince John. As he won the contest, the false king unmasked him, arrested him, and sentenced him to death.

"Please, no!" Maid Marian pleaded with Prince John. Confessing her love, she begged for Robin's life to be spared.

"Marian, my darling," Robin declared, "I love you

more than life itself."

The Prince refused to listen, but Little John would not let Robin down. With a knife pressed to Prince John's back, he forced the tyrant to release his friend. As the crowd cheered, Robin and Maid Marian embraced, but it wasn't long before the Sheriff of Nottingham figured out what was happening.

Quickly, Little John threw a sword toward Robin. While fending off soldiers, the archer swept Maid Marian off her feet and asked her to marry him. "Darling, I thought you'd never ask," she answered happily. Even Lady Kluck joined the fight against the soldiers, and they all escaped to Sherwood Forest.

Together again, Maid Marian and Robin Hood kissed in the romance of a night filled with fireflies. Offering a ring made from flowers, Robin pledged his love to her and the two walked back to camp hand in hand.

Their merriment did not last long, however. Prince John was angry about being humiliated. Tripling the taxes, he ordered the Sheriff to arrest all who could not

pay. Sadly, the prison filled quickly. Even Friar Tuck was arrested.

Robin Hood and

Little John decided it was time to stage a jailbreak. They knew the Sheriff would be on alert, but Robin was a master of disguise. In no time, he had fooled the guards and lulled the Sheriff to sleep, stealing his keys. As Little John released the prisoners, Robin crept into Prince John's bedroom and removed every last bag of gold.

Soon after, the rightful king,

Richard, returned and sent Prince John and his servants to prison. As the friends all gathered to celebrate the joyful wedding of Robin Hood and Maid Marian, Nottingham was a happy, peaceful town once again.

# THE
# LION KING II
# SIMBA'S · PRIDE

## LOVE WITHSTANDS ANYTHING

Kiara was warned never to go to the Outlands, but her father wouldn't tell her why. What could be so terrible? Kiara wondered curiously. As soon as her faithful guardians, Timon and Pumbaa, were distracted by

their favorite pastime of eating bugs, she crept away and ventured to the forbidden land.

There she met another lion cub. The two cubs helped each other cross a dangerous river full of crocodiles. Exhilarated by the adventure, Kiara exclaimed, "We make a good team!" With admiration she smiled at Kovu. "You were really brave," she told him.

He looked at her curiously. His mother, Zira, had always taught him that Pride

Landers couldn't be trusted, yet this lioness had saved him from the crocodile's teeth at least once.

"Yeah, you were pretty brave, too," Kovu admitted.

Happily, Kiara began to prance around him. She was laughing and wanted to play, but Kovu didn't understand.

He had never played tag. Just as Kiara began to make him smile and laugh, their parents arrived with bared teeth!

Kiara's father, Simba, was an enemy of Kovu's mother.

Because Zira was loyal to Scar, who had murdered

Simba's father, the Lion King had banished her to the

Outlands. Focused on revenge, she was raising Kovu to

hate. Her plan was to overthrow Simba and make her son the new King.

"Take your cub and get out!" Simba ordered. As Kovu and Kiara were separated, the friends sadly whispered

good-bye.

It was not until they were fully grown that the two saw each other again. Kiara

was a beautiful young lioness out on her first hunt. She had made her father promise not to interfere, but Simba was protective of his only daughter. As usual, he sent Timon and Pumbaa to watch over her . . . from a distance.

When Kiara came upon Timon and Pumbaa during her chase, she felt betrayed and angry. Wanting to prove that she could manage on her own, she raced away to hunt in the Outlands. Unaware that the Outsiders were watching her every move, she fell into their trap easily.

Quickly Zira and her followers set the plains on fire, surrounding Kiara. The young lioness ran until she fell unconscious. It was then that Kovu appeared. Trained to avenge Scar, he rescued the Princess only to get closer to his goal of killing Simba. He was ready for anything . . . except falling in love.

"Thanks for saving me," Kiara said after Simba reluctantly allowed Kovu to return with her to Pride Rock. She was happy to have him back in her life and she unwittingly distracted Kovu from his mission. Leading him away from her father, Kiara asked him to impress her with his expertise in stalking.

As Kovu showed her how to pounce quietly, they ran into Timon and Pumbaa. The silly animals were trying to rid their feeding ground

of pesky birds. "Lend a voice?" asked Timon. With a roar,

Kiara gave chase.

"Why are we doing this?" asked Kovu, puzzled. "For

fun!" answered Kiara. She showed Kovu the joy of

laughter, and he was exhilarated by the new experience.

Even after being chased by angry hippos he was happier than he had ever been. "What a blast!" he shouted, smiling at Kiara. By accident, the two bumped noses bashfully. "You're okay, kid!" said Timon.

That night Kovu and Kiara lay on the grass looking at the stars. "Do you think Scar's up there?" Kovu asked tentatively. "He wasn't my father, but he is a part of me."

Kiara knew he was troubled and tried to comfort her friend, but he pulled away. Confused, Kovu wasn't sure if he

should follow his mother's plan or follow his heart.

Nearby, the wise baboon, Rafiki, was watching. Leading the two lions to a place he called Upendi, Rafiki placed them in a boat. As Kovu watched Kiara during the wild ride, he gave in to his feelings for her. Kissing and laughing, Kiara guessed, "Upendi means love, doesn't it?"

Deciding not to follow in Scar's footsteps, Kovu made peace with Simba. But unawares, he and Simba were ambushed by the Outsiders. "No!" yelled Kovu, but it was too late. Simba believed he was responsible for the setup, and he exiled Kovu.

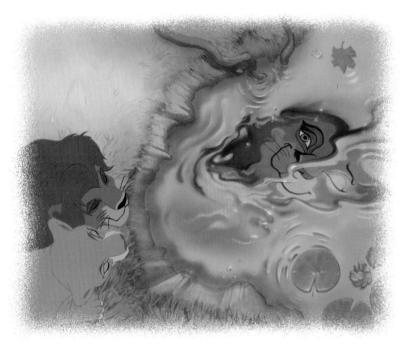

Heartbroken, Kiara knew that Kovu couldn't have been responsible for the ambush. Running away, she joined Kovu in the ashes of the fire.

"Hey, look! We are one," Kovu said looking at their reflection together in the water. As the wind blew the ashes away to reveal grass underneath, they knew their love could survive anything. Racing back to the Pride Lands, Kiara put an end to the war. "We are one!" she declared.

With peace settling over Pride Rock once more, Simba accepted Kovu's relationship with Kiara. Together, they joined the King and Queen for a celebration of unity.

# Disney's
# OLIVER
# & Company

## FRIENDS IN NEED

The orphaned kitten left alone in New York City didn't stand much of a chance. But a streetwise dog named Dodger had taken pity on the poor kitten.

The kitten was thankful to the dog. Dodger had protected him from vicious Dobermans and accepted him

as a part of the gang. Tito, Einstein, and Rita were glad to

have a new friend, and the master of the boat, Fagin, had

been kind and gentle, reading a story while petting the

kitten in his lap.

Happily the kitten curled up next to Dodger for the

night. As the dog watched the kitten sleeping beside him, he felt a protective bond and smiled tenderly at his new friend.

The next day the group set out to help Fagin. The poor man owed money to a gangster, and the loyal dogs would do whatever they could to lend a paw. Splitting up to do their work, Dodger told Tito to

keep his eye on

the kitten.

Ready for

adventure, the kitten

followed the

Chihuahua into an

expensive car. As

Tito tried to remove

the car stereo, the kitten jumped on the dashboard

nervously, hitting the ignition and blasting Tito out.

Scared, the kitten tried to hide, but a little girl named

Jenny leaned from the backseat to comfort him. As she

cuddled him, the kitten felt happier than he ever had

before. "I'm going to take you home," she promised him.

Lovingly, Jenny carried the kitten into her fancy Fifth

Avenue apartment. Naming him Oliver and making him a

special meal, she promised, "I'll take good care of you."

Together they played and practiced piano. Jenny

bought him a beautiful silver bowl and a collar with

a shiny name tag. She had been upset when her parents

said they wouldn't be home for her birthday, but now

she wasn't so lonely anymore. Oliver was just the friend she needed.

At school the next day Jenny was excited about the kitten waiting for her at home. Little did she know that Dodger and the gang were sneaking him out of the town

house while she

was away.

Proud of their

rescue, Dodger let

Oliver out of the

bag when they

returned to the

boat. "You're home

now," he told the kitten proudly. Oliver wasn't pleased. "I

was happy there," he said sadly. "I want to go back."

Crushed, Dodger reacted angrily. "Leave then!" he

said harshly, nodding toward the door. Oliver was sorry

that he had hurt his friend, but knew he belonged with

Jenny. Apologetically, he started to leave when Fagin

appeared. Noticing Oliver's expensive license, the

desperate man came up with an idea to ransom the kitten

in hopes of

exchanging Oliver

for the money

he needed to

pay his debt.

Unfortunately,

Jenny received the

note. Heartbroken,

the little girl set out to find Oliver. With her vain and

spoiled dog, Georgette, she carried her piggy bank and

followed the map Fagin had written, but it was confusing

and she got lost. When the gang found Jenny she was

scared and crying. "I'm trying to get my kitten back," she told Fagin.

Ashamed, he returned Oliver to her, but the gangster had been watching. The little girl was worth more money than the kitten, he thought. The gangster raced by in his black limousine, pulling her through the window.

Oliver was distraught. "We'll get her back," promised Dodger. Teaming up together, the group made a daring

rescue, escaping from the gangster's warehouse with Jenny. However, the evil man had a faster car than Fagin's three-wheel motorbike. He caught Jenny by the hand, but Oliver courageously jumped on the car, biting the gangster. Fagin saved the little girl and Dodger leaped

to protect Oliver, fighting the Dobermans on the back of the limousine.

Finally the chase ended when the gangster sped off an unfinished bridge. Dodger and Oliver jumped off just in time. Quickly, Fagin returned to get them, but as Jenny lifted Oliver he was unconscious. They all looked sorrowfully at the brave kitten just as he opened his eyes.

"Oliver!" cried Jenny swinging him around joyfully. The little girl embraced him happily as Oliver purred in her arms. When Jenny celebrated her birthday she invited all her animal friends, and Fagin, too. They had a party fit for a princess.

# DISNEY'S

# TARZAN®

## You'll Always Be in My Heart

Young Tarzan looked with anguish at his reflection in the water and covered his face with mud. He desperately wanted to fit in with the other gorillas. Why am I different? he thought. He wanted to look like the rest of his family. He wanted to move as surely through

the trees and be as

strong, too.

When his mother,

Kala, found him, she

felt his pain. Trying

to comfort Tarzan,

she showed him that

they had the same hands and that her heartbeat was the

same as his. Enveloped in his mother's hug, the boy felt a

new strength and determination. "I'll be the best ape

ever!" he promised.

True to his word, Tarzan grew into an adult with great

skills. He imitated the jungle animals and wrestled with his best friend, Terk, until he developed ways to overcome her superior strength. He swung from trees with great speed. With a spear he had invented, he was even able to rescue Kerchak, the gorilla leader, from the vicious leopard, Sabor.

Proudly, he earned acceptance from his peers. Up until the day he met Jane, Tarzan had put his doubts and miseries behind him.

When gunshots rang out one day, Tarzan investigated

the strange noise. He was surprised to come upon three

strange creatures. Clayton, a hunter, was leading

Professor Porter and his daughter, Jane, on an expedition

to study gorillas.

When Jane stayed behind to sketch a young baboon, Tarzan rescued her from the baboon's angry family. After the terrifying chase, Jane tried to back away from the wild man, but he came closer to her, touching her hands with a look of fascination. They were just like his! When he listened to her heartbeat and laid her head against his

own chest, she was afraid, but she realized that he wasn't going to hurt her. Though his eyes were intense, his smile was kind and his manner gentle.

"Tarzan," he spoke, pointing to himself, and they began to communicate. Slowly, Tarzan learned Jane's language. Visiting the human camp, he was fascinated with pictures of people and places. Everything was new to Tarzan. Jane and her father, excited by his enthusiasm, became Tarzan's teachers.

"I've never seen him so happy," Tantor said to Terk as the friends watched Tarzan pick flowers for Jane. He could not stop thinking about her. The bond between them had become more than a simple attraction. One morning, Tarzan arrived at the campsite but was surprised to learn that it was time for Jane to leave.

"Jane. Stay!" pleaded Tarzan as he handed her the

flowers. Crying, Jane ran away. She was as upset as Tarzan about her leaving.

Nearby, Clayton was forming a wicked plan. Wanting to capture the gorillas, he made Tarzan believe that Jane might stay if she could meet the apes.

Jane and her father were thrilled when Tarzan brought them to his family. Joyfully, Jane watched Tarzan talking to the young gorillas. "Can you teach me?" Jane asked.

Gently, Tarzan helped her form the gorilla words. As the apes reacted noisily, Jane wanted to know what he had taught her to say. "Jane stays with Tarzan," he told her, but she shook her head.

That evening Tarzan sat in a tree watching the distant boat anchored offshore. He wasn't sure what he should

do. Kala had told him he was her son, but he looked like the humans. Where did he belong?

Then his mother found him. Silently she led him to

the tree house where she had found him years ago.

An old picture of his human family was still on the floor.

"I just want you to be happy . . . whatever you decide,"

she told him.

Moments later, he had dressed in his father's clothes. "No matter where I go you will always be my mother," said Tarzan as he headed toward the beach. "And you will always be in my heart," she replied.

Sadly, Tantor

and Terk watched the dinghy pull away. "We didn't even get to say good-bye," said the elephant regretfully. Then a wild cry of despair reached shore. Tarzan was in trouble!

Quickly Tantor
and Terk swam to
the ship where
Clayton had locked
their friend in the
hold. Bravely
fighting off thugs,
they released

Tarzan and Jane. "I thought I was never gonna see you

again!" sobbed Terk.

Calling the jungle animals for help, they battled

Clayton and his men, but Kerchak was shot trying to save

Tarzan. "Forgive me for not understanding that you have

always been one of us," the dying gorilla told Tarzan.

"Take care of our family . . . my son."

Even though she had said a tearful good-bye to Tarzan,

once Jane was on the boat she realized that she loved him

too much to leave. Splashing back to shore, she embraced him joyfully, as friends and family cheered. "Oo-oo-ee-eh-ou," said Jane. "Jane stays with Tarzan!"